Lee Aucoin, *Creative Director*
Jamey Acosta, *Senior Editor*
Heidi Fiedler, *Editor*
Produced and designed by
Denise Ryan & Associates
Illustration © Claire Chrystall
Rachelle Cracchiolo, *Publisher*

Teacher Created Materials

5301 Oceanus Drive
Huntington Beach, CA 92649-1030
http://www.tcmpub.com
Paperback: ISBN: 978-1-4333-5534-9
Library Binding: ISBN: 978-1-4807-1702-2
© 2014 Teacher Created Materials

The Glass Slippers

Written by Sharon Callen

Illustrated by Claire Chrystall

Once upon a time, there was a kind and beautiful girl named Cinder. She had two stepsisters who were not kind or beautiful.

3

Cinder's stepsisters liked to dress up in grand clothes and go to grand parties. Cinder always had to stay home and clean the house.

Sometimes, she wished she could dress in grand clothes and go to grand parties. But she never complained.

One day, an invitation came from Prince Charming. The stepsisters were invited to a party at the palace!

On the day of the party, the stepsisters dressed in their grandest clothes and left Cinder to clean the house while they were gone.

"Enjoy the cleaning," they laughed. "Be sure to do a grand job!"

You're Invited
to
The Grand Ball
Where: The Palace
When: Friday Night
Dress: Grand Clothes

Just after they left for the party, there was a flash of light. Cinder's fairy godmother landed on the floor of the kitchen.

"Oh! Something went wrong," Fairy Godmother said, as she stood up. "What a mess I've made!" Then, with a swish of her wand, the house was clean.

8

"I'm here to help you get ready for the party," said Fairy Godmother to Cinder.

"First, you will need a beautiful gown."

Swish!

"And we must do your hair."

Swish! Swish!

"And now for something very special. A pair of grand glass slippers!"

Swish! Swish! Swish!

"Oh! That didn't work," said Fairy Godmother. "Those heels are much too high. I'm afraid I'm just learning how to make glass slippers."

So, she tried again.

Swish!

The slippers were much too big.

Swish! Swish!

The slippers were much too small.

Swish! Swish! Swish!

The slippers were perfect. "Oh my!"
said Cinder. "Glass slippers with wings!"

13

"These slippers are very special. They will fly you to the party. And they will bring you home at midnight. You are kind and beautiful. I hope you enjoy the party," said Fairy Godmother.

Then, with a swish of her wand, the glass slippers flapped their wings and carried Cinder to the palace.

14

15

Cinder danced all night with Prince Charming. But when the clock struck midnight, the slippers flapped their wings, and something went wrong.

Cinder began flying around and around the room, faster and faster!

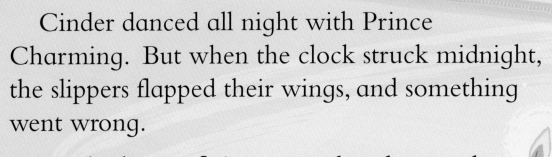

17

Suddenly, there was a flash of light and a loud noise. Fairy Godmother landed on the ballroom floor!

"Something went wrong," she said as she stood up. Then, she waved her wand and brought Cinder safely back to the floor.

Cinder felt very dizzy. But the Prince said, "You are so kind and beautiful." He led her to the throne.

21

"No, she's not," laughed the stepsisters. "We are far more kind and beautiful." But Fairy Godmother knew they were not kind, so she swished her wand three times, and a different kind of slipper appeared on the stepsisters' feet. These glass slippers had wheels!

23

The stepsisters skated around and around the room, going faster and faster. They could not stop.

And who knows, they may still be there!